HENRY
the Dog with No Tail

KATE FEIFFER
ILLUSTRATED BY JULES FEIFFER

A Paula Wiseman Book
SIMON & SCHUSTER BOOKS FOR YOUNG READERS
NEW YORK • LONDON • TORONTO • SYDNEY

SIMON & SCHUSTER BOOKS FOR YOUNG READERS

An imprint of Simon & Schuster Children's Publishing Division

1230 Avenue of the Americas, New York, New York 10020

Text copyright © 2007 by Kate Feiffer

Illustrations copyright © 2007 by Jules Feiffer

SIMON & SCHUSTER BOOKS FOR YOUNG READERS is a trademark of Simon & Schuster, Inc.

Book design by Lizzy Bromley

The text for this book is set in Kis.

The illustrations for this book are rendered with charcoal pencil and watercolor.

Manufactured in China

10 9 8 7 6 5 4 3 2 1

Library of Congress Cataloging-in-Publication Data

Feiffer, Kate.

Henry the dog with no tail / Kate Feiffer ; illustrated by Jules Feiffer. — 1st ed.

p. cm.

"A Paula Wiseman book."

Summary: Envious of the other dogs that have tails, Henry goes in search of a tail of his own, but in the end he decides he is happy the way he is.

ISBN-13: 978-1-4169-1614-7 (hardcover)

ISBN-10: 1-4169-1614-8 (hardcover)

[1. Australian shepherd dog—Fiction. 2. Dogs—Fiction. 3. Tail—Fiction. 4. Identity—Fiction. 5. Humorous stories.] I. Feiffer, Jules, ill. II. Title.

PZ7.F33346He 2007

[E]—dc22

2006013418

For Chris
-K. F.

For Jenny
-J. F.

Henry wanted one thing in life.

He wanted a tail.

Henry was a dog with no tail. And this made him sad.
All the other dogs he knew had tails.

His best friend, Grady, a black Labrador, had a great big black tail that he swung
like a baseball bat and chased like a cat.

His friend Pip, a pug, could do tricks with her tail. She could twist it and curl it. Pip liked to put on shows for the other dogs. She'd ask the dogs in the audience to bark to ten, and before they were done, she had tied her tail in a bow.

And then there was Larry. Larry, whose real name was Larrissima, was a prize-winning poodle whose tail stuck straight up in the air and had a big puffy ball stuck to the end of it.

Henry didn't care if he had a long or thin or curly or puffy tail. He didn't care what kind of tail he had. Henry moped around his house feeling sorry for himself. He moped and he moped.

His owners saw how sad he was, so they told him he should go find a tail.
Henry thought this was a fine idea and left home in search of a tail.

And naturally, when a dog goes in search of a tail,
he goes to the tailor's.

"Hello," said Henry.
"Hello," said the tailor.

"I am here for a tail," said Henry.
"As you can see, I do not have one.
Perhaps you have an extra."
"I don't have tails here. But I could try
to make you one," replied the tailor.

The tailor worked all day and all
night and made a tail for Henry.

The tailor buttoned it on and Henry went on his way.
Henry wanted to show off his new tail, so he went to
the park.

"Look," he said. "I've got a new tail."

"Wow. Neat. Cool,"
said Grady.
"Does it do any
tricks?" asked Pip.

Henry ran around in a circle and jumped over his tail.

The first time he did a high jump.

Then he did a long jump.

Then he ran backward and jumped.

He did a spin jump,

a low jump,

and a leap jump.

Then he . . .

tripped.

"Guess what? Dogs don't trip over real tails," said Larrissima.

"I think your tricks are neat," said Grady.

"Sometimes tricks take practice," added Pip.

"It doesn't look like a real tail to me," said Larry. "If that's a real tail, then wag it."

Henry tried to wag his tail.
But it wouldn't wag.

"I told you that wasn't a tail,"
scoffed Larry. "It's a fake!"

Henry left the park feeling miserable.
His new tail was too long, and worst
of all, it didn't wag. What good was a
tail that didn't wag?

So Henry went to the wagon maker and asked,
"Can you make my tail wag?"

But the wagon maker said, "I don't make things wag.
I make wagons."

Henry bought a wagon from the wagon maker.

He filled his wagon with food and water and left town, vowing not to return until his new tail wagged. He traveled for three days and three nights. He climbed mountains and walked around lakes.

On the fourth day he ended up in New York City's Battery Park.
It was full of batteries.

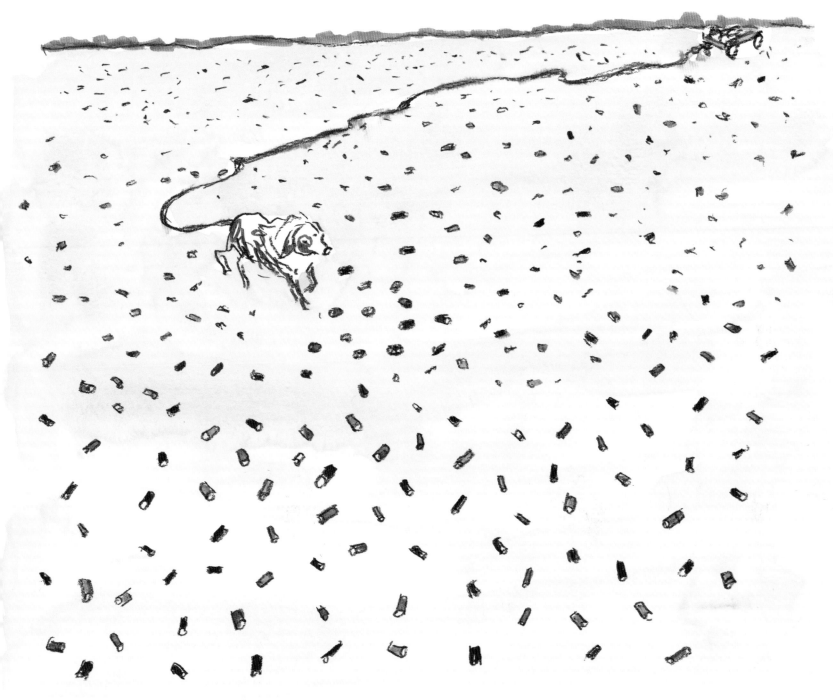

Henry decided to put one on his tail.
And . . .

His tail started to wag.

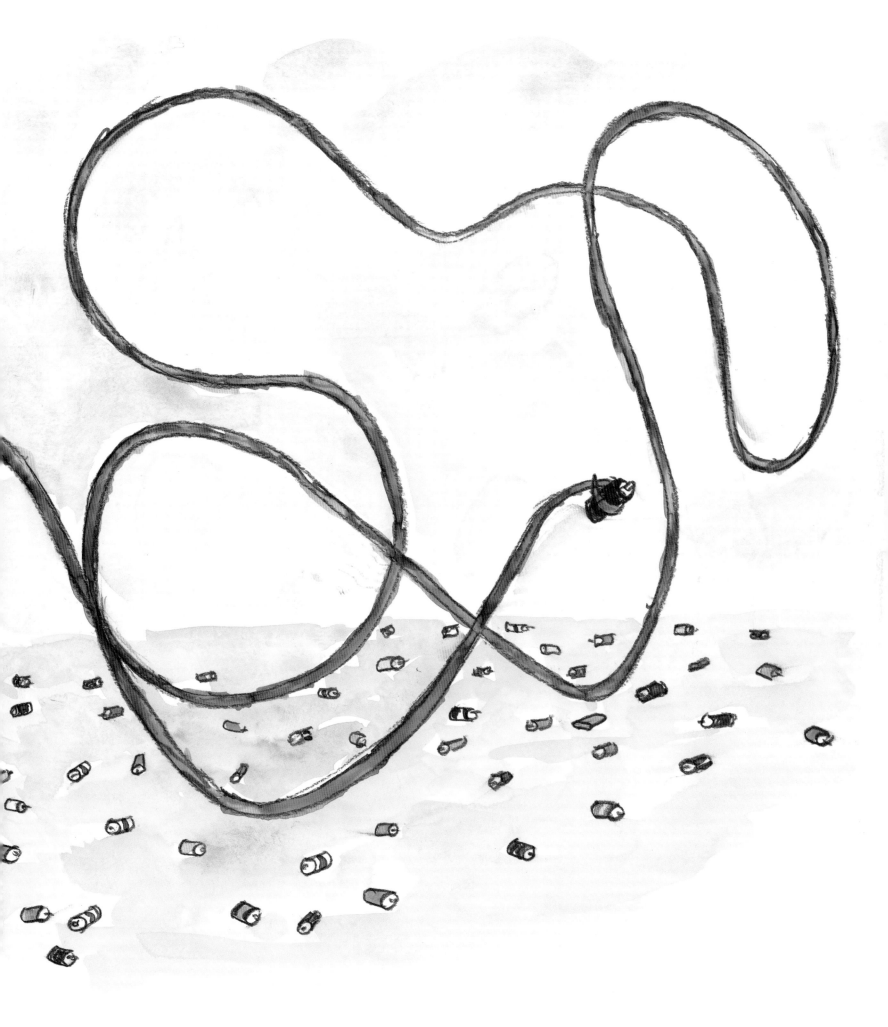

Henry packed up his wagon and headed home.

His tail started wagging so fast it was hard to walk.
So he ran. Then his tail started wagging so fast that
it was hard to run. So he sat down and his tail pushed
him the rest of the way.
"Look," said Henry, "my tail wags."
"Wow. Neat. Cool," said Grady.

"Harrumph," scoffed Larry.
"You can be in my show," said an excited Pip.

Which was good because Henry's tail was wagging so fast it lifted him off the ground and threw him along like a Frisbee.

Since not many dogs have tails that can toss them across a field,
Pip was sure the show would be a great success.
She called together all the dogs.

After finishing her act, Pip announced her new partner.

"Introducing Henry, the dog with the **super tail**.

It's unlike any tail anywhere at any time in any place.

Please put your paws together for Henryyyyyy."

The dogs put paw to paw and barked a round of appaws. At this point Henry was supposed to fly onto the stage.

But he didn't.
Instead he shouted, "I'm up here!"

All the dogs looked up. Henry was in the air, flying like a helicopter.

Grady and the other dogs thought this was a pretty cool
trick and shouted, "Higher! Higher! Higher!"

But Henry didn't want to go higher. He wanted to go lower. He wanted to be on the ground chasing balls, not up in the air dodging birds. Henry was scared.

He grabbed on to a branch at the very top of a tree and held on as tight as he could.

"Higher! Higher! Higher!" chanted the dogs down below.

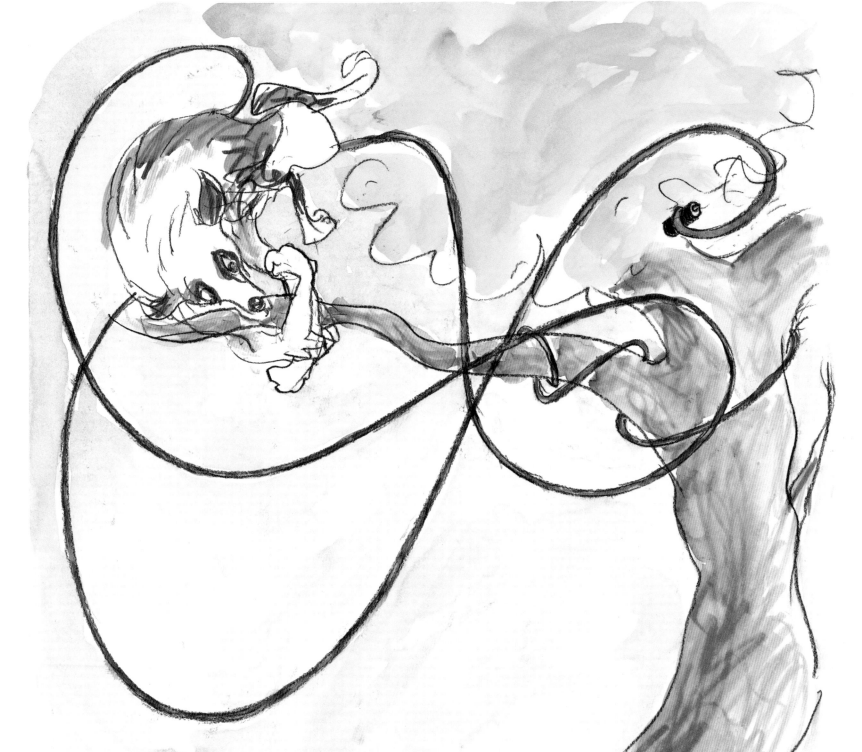

All the dogs, that is, but one.
"Take the battery off of your tail," yelled Larry.

Even though it was Larry's idea, Henry knew it was a good idea.
He took the battery off of his tail and . . . it stopped wagging.

Then he took off
his tail and hung it
from a branch on
the tree.

Henry, the dog
with no tail,

carefully

climbed

down

the

tree.

"Wow. Neat. Cool," said Grady.

"What a show," exclaimed Pip.

"You know, I guess you're not so bad without a tail," conceded Larry.

Henry agreed.

"I think my days of having a tail are behind me," he said.

To this day Henry's tail remains on the tree, flapping like a flag in the wind. And to this day Henry, the dog with no tail, is very happy that he's a dog with no tail and a tale to tell.